Maui Tames the Sun

A play by Alan Trussell-Cullen based on a traditional Maori legend

Illustrated by Tracie Grimwood

Characters

Narrator
(Storyteller)

Maui

Sun
(Tama)

Warrior 1   Warrior 2   Warrior 3   Warrior 4

Flax Weavers

Carvers

Food Gatherers

Children

Turn to page **29** for Sound and Stage Tips

Maui Tames the Sun

Narrator: Long, long ago, when the world was new and strange, the sun did not travel slowly across the sky as it does today.

Oh no! Tama, the sun creature, would leap up from his deep cave in the east …

(The Sun leaps up from his cave.)

And laugh at the world and all its creatures below.

Sun: Ha, ha, ha! So you want my light?
So you want my warmth?
Well catch it while you can!
Ha, ha, ha, ha!

Narrator: And then he would rush across the sky like a mad thing.

Sun: Ha, ha, ha, ha!

Narrator: And dive behind the mountains of the west. In so doing, he would plunge the world into darkness again. The result was the days were ever so short and no one had time to do anything properly. Everyone complained.

All the People: (*They mutter phrases like …*)
Too short!
Where does the day go?
That sun is always misbehaving!
This is terrible!
We never get anything done.

Narrator: The weavers of the flax complained.

**Flax
Weavers:**   How can we weave our flax into
baskets and mats and fishing nets
when the days are so short?

All the People: (*Nodding at the Flax Weavers.*) We know.

Narrator: The carvers complained.

Carvers: How can we carve our houses and spears and canoes when the days are so short?

All the People: *(Nodding at the Carvers.)* That's right.

Narrator: The people who gathered all the food complained.

Food Gatherers: How can we catch our fish and dig the soil and plant our kumara when the days are so short?

All the People: *(Nodding at the Food Gatherers.)* That's true.

Narrator: The children complained.

Children: How can we fly our kites and spin our tops when the days are so short?

All the People: Someone ought to do something.

Narrator:	But no one did anything.
	(The Flax Weavers, Carvers, Food Gatherers and Children all walk around muttering and complaining to each other. The noise becomes louder.)
All the People:	Where does the day go? The days are too short! There's no time for anything! That wicked sun!
	(Maui enters. He listens to the people complaining and frowns.)
Narrator:	*(Over the top of the babble.)* Finally, Maui grew tired of hearing everyone complain.
	(Maui becomes angry. Then he puts his hands over his ears. Finally, he cannot stand it any longer.)

Maui: Quiet!

(The people stop and stare at Maui.)

All this complaining!

I am Maui the wise one. I am Maui the shrewd one. Maui the cunning one. Maui the trickster. Maui the curious one. Maui the one who always asks lots of questions! Maui the magical one!

But no one calls me Maui the patient one who loves listening to people complaining!

(Maui glares at the people. They back away from him a little.)

Maui:	If the days are too short, it is because the sun goes too fast across the sky.
Chief Carver:	We know that, Maui. *(Everyone nods.)* But what can we do about it?
All the People:	Yes! That's right! What can we do about it?
Maui:	Simple! *(Everyone is quiet and listening again.)* We can catch the sun and make him go slower. *(The people begin to laugh.)*
Flax Weavers:	Catch the sun?
Carvers:	Make him go slower?

Food Gatherers: That's ridiculous! Ordinary people can't do that.

Maui: You forget. I am Maui.
I am not an ordinary person. Help me, and I will catch the sun and make him go more slowly across the sky.

(The people look at each other for a second, and then they begin to nod and agree.)

All the People: We could give it a try.
He has done some amazing things in the past.
All right.
We'll help!

Maui: Flax Weavers?

Flax Weavers: Yes, Maui?

Maui: I need you to weave the finest flax into the strongest net you have ever made!

Flax Weavers: *(Becoming excited.)* Yes!

Maui: Carvers?

Carvers: Yes, Maui?

Maui: I need you to carve a giant spear and the largest club you have ever made!

Carvers: *(Becoming excited.)* Yes!

Maui: I need four strong warriors to come with me to catch the sun.

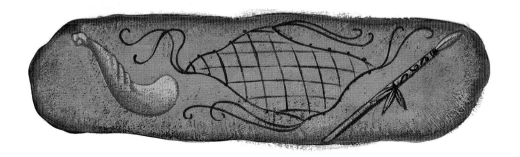

Warrior 1:	I'll come with you, Maui!
Warrior 2:	And I will!
Warrior 3:	And I will!
Warrior 4:	And I will!
Maui:	And we shall need food and clothing for the journey.
Flax Weavers:	We shall weave you clothes!
Food Gatherers:	We shall prepare the food!
Children:	And we'll help everyone!
Narrator:	So the people began to work.

(They all begin to mime their tasks.)
The flax weavers wove a giant net.

(The Flax Weavers mime working on a great rope net.)

Narrator:	The carvers made a giant spear and a giant club.

(The Carvers mime the carving of a giant spear and club.)

Food was gathered and prepared for the warriors.

(The Food Gatherers mime the digging of kumara and catching of fish.)

And the children watched, and helped where they could.

(The Children move around the groups, watching and helping.)

When everything was ready, the warriors set out on a long journey to Te Rua-o-te-Ra, the cave where the sun hides by night.

(The Warriors are ready. They receive the club and spear from the Carvers and the net from the Flax Weavers. They carry the flax baskets of food. They set out on their journey. The people wave goodbye.)

Narrator:	They journeyed for many days. And because they did not want Tama, the sun creature, to know that they were coming, they travelled by night and slept by day.

(The Warriors and Maui travel about the stage, moving through an imaginary forest with stealth and care to avoid the sun seeing them.)

And then, one night, they came to the dark, dark cave where the sun spent the night.

Maui: Shh! Quietly brothers! The sun is sleeping. We do not want to disturb him. First, we must place the net over the mouth of the cave.

(The Warriors struggle to place the net over the mouth of the cave. They grunt and strain and whisper to each other.)

Warrior 1: Toss the rope.

Warrior 2: I have my end of the net.

Warrior 3: I'm pulling! It's heavy!

Warrior 4: It's nearly there.

Warrior 1: The net is ready, Maui.

Maui: Good. Now you must hold fast onto the ropes because the sun is very strong and he will struggle to escape.

Narrator: The warriors waited and waited. Finally, the night passed and morning came. The sun awoke. He stretched.

Sun:	Ahh.
Maui:	*(whispering)* Hold tight, brothers!
Sun:	Another day. Oh me! Oh my! Another rush across the sky. Here I go! *(The Sun gets caught in the net held by the Warriors.)* Woe! What is this? I seem to be tangled in something!
Narrator:	The sun pushed on Maui's net.
Sun:	Aghhh!
Narrator:	The sun pulled on Maui's net.
Sun:	Aghhh!
Narrator:	The sun heaved and hauled and shoved and yanked.
Sun:	Agh! Agh! Agh! Aghhh!

Maui:	Hold fast, brothers.
Warriors 1, 2, 3 and 4:	We're trying to, Maui.
Sun:	Do I hear voices? Who has dared do this to me?
Maui:	It is I! Maui!
Sun:	Maui?
Maui:	I have caught you in my net. Now you must do as I tell you.
Sun:	Never, Maui! I will break your puny net.
Maui:	Then I must teach you a lesson so you will behave better in the future.
Sun:	What have you there?
Maui:	A giant spear carved by our best carvers.

Sun:	Ha, ha, ha! Do you think I am frightened of a little stick?
Narrator:	And the sun spat out a tongue of fire that snapped the giant spear like a twig.
FX:	*(Spear breaking.)*
	(The Sun lunges at the spear through the net. There is a flash of light and the spear seems to break in the middle. The Warriors gasp.)
Maui:	You will be sorry, Tama. You may have destroyed our spear, but our finest carvers carved this giant greenstone club.
Sun:	Ha, ha, ha! Do you think I am frightened of a little piece of stone? Take that, you little whippersnapper!
Narrator:	And the sun spat out a tongue of fire so hot that it made the stone glow red-hot. Maui had to drop it before his hand was burnt.
	(The Sun lunges at the club. There is a flash of light and the club glows. Maui drops it.)

Sun:	Now will you let me go?
Maui:	No, Tama! Not just yet. You force me to use my magic.
Narrator:	And Maui put his hand into his cloak and pulled out a curved piece of white bone. It glowed in the early morning light. The warriors gasped with pain and fear.
Warriors 1, 2, 3 and 4:	Ah Maui! It is blinding!

Sun:	Ha, ha, ha! What have you got now, little boy? Another toy for me to destroy?
Maui:	This is no toy! My great-great-grandmother gave this to me. It is bone. Special bone. Magic bone. I do not even have to hit you with it for you to feel its power. All I have to do is touch you.
Sun:	Touch away!
Maui:	Like this. *(Maui touches the Sun with the bone. The Sun pulls back in pain.)*
Sun:	Yaaa!
Maui:	And like this.
Sun:	Yaaa!
Maui:	And like this.

Sun: No! Stop! Stop! No more!

Maui: Then will you do what we ask?

Sun: No! Never! I don't take any orders from anyone.

Maui: Then I will touch you again.

Sun: Yaaa! No!

Maui: And again.

Sun: No! Stop! I give up!

Maui: Then hear me, oh sun creature. And hear me well.

The people of my world are tired of the way you sprint across the sky.

Our weavers have no time to weave.

Our carvers have no time to carve.

Our gatherers of food have no time to fish or to grow our kumara.

Our children have no time to play.

From now on, you must take your time as you cross the heavens.

You must be like an old man who has time to dawdle.

You must smell every flower as you go and peep into every deep valley and listen to every birdsong.

That way, the days will be long enough for people to work and play and do all that they have to do.

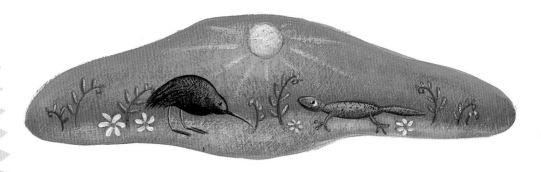

Sun:	Do I have any choice, oh Maui the powerful one?
Maui:	No, sun creature! You must agree by the time we count to five, or else I will let you feel the power of my magic bone again. One!
Sun:	But I don't want to.
Maui and Warriors 1, 2, 3 and 4:	Two!
Sun:	But I don't need to.
Maui and Warriors 1, 2, 3 and 4:	Three!
Sun:	You can't make me.
Maui and Warriors 1, 2, 3 and 4:	Four!

Sun: All right! All right! I give in! I'll go more slowly across the sky.

Maybe it would be rather nice to see what is going on in the world below.

I'll be able to know everyone's secrets.

I'll know what people are cooking.

I'll see what people are catching when they are fishing.

I'll see the children's kites fluttering in the breeze and their tops spinning round and round and round.

Maui: Then we will let you go, Tama.

But just in case you ever try to speed up again, we will leave our ropes tied to you so that we can quickly catch hold of them and slow you down again.

Sun: All right! All right! See how slowly I am going?

(The Sun begins to cross the stage ever so slowly.)

I am a snail crawling across your sky.

A turtle.

A lazy child who does not want to do chores, so he dallies and dawdles and daydreams.

Narrator: And so Maui and his warriors returned to his people.

(Maui and the Warriors return to the people who applaud and bow before them.)
And they all gave them a hero's welcome.

All the People: **Ka whiti mai te ra**
Ka ora ai te tangata!

(The people return to their tasks, the Flax Weavers weave, the Carvers carve and the Food Gatherers dig for kumara and net for fish. The Children play. The Sun continues to slowly cross the stage.)

Narrator: From that day on, the sun moved slowly across the sky.
And everyone was grateful to Maui for giving them more time in the day.

(Everyone smiles and nods to Maui.)
The weavers could weave their flax mats and nets.

(The Flax Weavers mime weaving.)
The carvers could carve their beautiful carvings.

(The Carvers mime carving.)
The food gatherers could catch lots of fish and grow kumara in their gardens.

(The Food Gatherers mime fishing and digging for kumara.)

Narrator: And the children could play.

(The Children mime flying their kites and spinning their tops.)

And sometimes, oh listeners, when the sun is just rising or just setting, you can see what seem to be lines hanging down across the sky. Those are ropes that are left tied to the sun just in case he should ever misbehave again.

And that is why, to this day, my people call them Maui's ropes!

(The Sun has reached the other side of the stage. If you are using lighting, dim the stage to silhouette and then to blackout.)

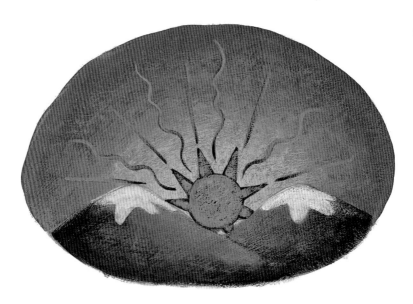

Sound and Stage Tips

About This Play

This play tells one of the favourite stories of the Maori people of New Zealand. You can read it with your friends or act it out in front of an audience. You could even record your reading and play it back as a radio play, or video-tape your performance so you can watch it on video and share it with others. Before you start reading, choose a part or parts you would like to read.

Besides the main characters, like Maui and the Narrator, this play also has groups of people, such as Carvers, Flax Weavers, Children and Food Gatherers. You will need at least fifteen people, so make sure you have enough readers for all the parts.

Reading the Play

It's a good idea to read the play through to yourself before you read it as part of a group. It is best to have your own book, as that will help you too. As you read the play through, think about each character and how they might feel in this situation. Think about how they might look and sound too. How are they behaving? What sort of voice might they have in the play?

Many of the characters have to mime actions in this play, like weaving fishing nets and digging to plant the kumara. Think about how you could perform these actions so that others would understand what you are doing.

Rehearsing the Play

Rehearse the play a few times before you perform it for others. There are times in this play when you may find you are part of a group that is expected to talk a lot and make a lot of noise. It is almost like a piece of music. When the people are complaining, for example, they will become louder and louder, but they must all stop at the same time when Maui tells them to be quiet. You might like to practise these group scenes several times.

Remember you are an actor as well as a reader. Your facial expressions and the way you stand and move are going to help your audience understand and enjoy the play.

Using Your Voice

Remember to speak out clearly and be careful not to read too quickly. Sometimes it helps to pause after you have said a line so that the audience has time to try to anticipate what might happen next.

Practise saying the traditional Maori words at the end of the play:

Ka whiti mai te ra
Ka ora ai te tangata.

This means:

Now that daylight has broken through
The people can rejoice.

Remember to look at the audience and at the other actors, making sure that everyone can hear what you are saying.

Creating Sound Effects (FX)

In *Maui Tames the Sun*, there are many places where the use of sound effects will help create extra atmosphere. You will need a sound to match the breaking of Maui's spear. A cymbal or snare drum might work well. Drumbeats could accompany the Warriors as they set out on their journey. You may also wish to add theme music or sounds for the Sun's movement across the sky and struggle in the net.

Sets and Props

Once you have read the play, make a list of the things you will need. Sometimes it is better to have no real props at all and use mime to help your audience imagine them. The net in this play is often better mimed in this way.

If you decide to make these props, use a branch or thin wood to make the spear. Maori warriors did not throw their spears, but used them for swinging and jabbing at the enemy. In the hands of a fierce warrior, the spear was a terrifying weapon. For this story, the spear needs to appear to snap. One way to do this is to cut your spear in half and hinge the two pieces together.

Costumes

Maori clothing was woven from flax, which is a strong, grass-like plant. Men and women wore a kind of apron around their waists made from specially treated strands of flax. Important people like Maui would have a special cloak made from flax and lined with fine bird feathers.

Have fun!

❦ Ideas for guided reading ❦

Learning objectives: investigate how settings and characters are built from small details; identify the main characteristics of the key characters, drawing on the text to justify views; prepare, read and perform playscripts; know the ways in which the adjectives can be made into verbs; comment constructively on plays and performance

Curriculum links: PE: Dance activities

Interest words: Maui, Tama, kumara, flax, Te Rua-o-te-Ra

Resources: tape recorder, whiteboard and pens

Casting: (1) Narrator (2) Maui (3) Sun (4) Warrior 1, Warrior 4 & the Flax Weavers (5) Warrior 2 & the Carvers (6) Warrior 3, the Food Gatherers & the Children (All) All the people

Getting started

- Explain to the children that this play is based around a Maori legend. Check that they know that Maori people are indigenous to New Zealand.

- Turn to p29 and read *About This Play* to the children.

- Encourage the children to browse through the play finding unusual words: *Maui, flax,* etc. and decide on their meanings (e.g. flax → grass-like plant). Discuss why some words may not be in the dictionary.

- Read through the characters on p2 and allocate roles.

Reading and responding

- Read the paragraph *Using your voice* on p30 and practise together the Maori words at the end of the play.

- Practise together the multiple voices on p5.

- Read from the beginning together and praise good expression.

- Discuss use of voices – which parts need to be asked as questions? Which parts need a louder voice? Encourage the children to look for punctuation such as question marks and exclamation marks.

Returning to the book

- Make a character sketch of Maui. What kind of person is he? Encourage children to look for evidence in the text, e.g. he is boastful because he says, *I am not an ordinary person.*